Little Wolf's New Home

The Langley School
Lower School

by April Maguire

illustrated by Laura J. Bryant

D0167451

Little Wolf had a
nice home in a den.
The den was warm and safe.

But the den was small,
and Little Wolf had lots
of brothers and sisters.
She wanted a bigger,
better home.

So Little Wolf went off
to look for a bigger,
better home.

She went to see
her friend, Blue Bird.

"Good morning, Blue Bird,"
said Little Wolf.
"I am looking
    for a new home."

"My home is in this tree,"
said Blue Bird.
"A tree is a good home."

Little Wolf liked Blue Bird.
But she did not like
Blue Bird's home.
The tree was too high.

"No, thanks," said Little Wolf.
"A tree is not the right home
for me."

So Little Wolf went to see
her friend, Bear.

"Hi, Bear," said Little Wolf.
"I am looking for
a new home."

"Well," said Bear.
"A cave is a good home."

Little Wolf liked Bear.
But Bear's home was
too dark.

"No, thanks," said Little Wolf.
"A cave is not the right
home for me."

Little Wolf walked on and on.
She walked by a river.

"Hello, Little Wolf,"
said Fish.

"Hello, Fish," Little Wolf said.

But Little Wolf kept walking.
She did not like Fish's home.
The river was too wet!

Little Wolf walked all day.
Soon it was dark.
Little Wolf was cold
and very sleepy.

She thought about the warm, safe den with her brothers and sisters.

Little Wolf ran home.

"I don't need a bigger, better home," she said. "My home is just right!"